J398.22 Bawden, Nina, 1925-
BAW   William Tell

82
85

82 00936

WILLIAM TELL

Pour Guillaume E. P.A.
For Kate and Tom and Lucy N.B.

also by Pascale Allamand

THE BOY AND HIS FRIEND THE BEAR
THE POP ROOSTER
THE CAMEL WHO LEFT THE ZOO
THE LITTLE GOAT IN THE MOUNTAINS
THE ANIMALS WHO CHANGED THEIR COLORS

Text copyright © 1981 by Nina Bawden
Illustrations © 1981 by Pascale Allamand

First published in Great Britain in 1981 by
Jonathan Cape Ltd.

Printed in Italy by New Interlitho, SpA, Milan

First U.S. Edition
1 2 3 4 5 6 7 8 9 10

Library of Congress Cataloging in Publication Data

Bawden, Nina, (date)
William Tell.

SUMMARY: A retelling of the story of William Tell,
who shot an apple from his son's head and ultimately
was responsible for the formation of the country of
Switzerland.
1. Tell, Wilhelm – Legends. 2. Legends – Switzerland.
[1. Tell, William. 2. Folklore – Switzerland]
I. Allamand, Pascale.
PZ8.1.B35Wi   398.2'2'09494 [E]   80–24786

ISBN 0–688–41985–2
ISBN 0–688–51985–7 (lib. bdg.)

WILLIAM TELL

Story told by Nina Bawden
Pictures by Pascale Allamand

LOTHROP, LEE & SHEPARD BOOKS NEW YORK

Long ago, in a time when soldiers wore suits of chain mail and men still went hunting with bows and arrows, there were three little countries in Europe called Schwytz, Uri, and Unterwald. This was in the heart of the Alps, on the borders of Austria, where the lakes were leaping with fish and the forests running with game, and the people could have been happy and prosperous. But from the dark castles on the high mountain slopes, the Austrian soldiers and bailiffs ruled over them harshly.

Every month, the Austrian bailiffs demanded a tax from the people. They had to take most of the fish they had caught, the game they had hunted, and the crops they had grown up the long hill to the castle. The soldiers and bailiffs grew fat and lazy and arrogant, and the people, thin and sullen and frightened.

The worst of the bailiffs was a cruel man called Gessler. Most of the people lived in wooden houses, but one farmer lived in a house built of stone, and this made Gessler jealous and angry. Why should this poor, ordinary farmer live in a nice, warm, stone house while he had to live in a draughty old castle? So one day he came with his soldiers and threw the poor farmer out of his home.

Everyone was afraid of Gessler, except for a brave hunter whose name was William Tell.

One morning, when William Tell was setting off with his son to the market, his wife tried to stop him. She said, "Oh, William, don't go to the village today. Gessler is sure to be there, and I am afraid of him."

But William Tell laughed and said, "I am not afraid of the bailiff! It is Gessler who should be afraid of me — and of my good bow and swift arrows!"

Gessler was not only jealous and cruel, he was proud. So proud that he had stuck his hat on a pole in the market-place and instructed his soldiers to make all the people salute it. This made William Tell very angry. He refused to salute a man's hat! So the soldiers arrested him and summoned the bailiff.

Gessler said, "How dare you ignore my hat, you insolent fellow! You will have to learn who is master! I hear that you boast of your skill with a bow. Well, now you can show me how clever you are. You must shoot an apple off the head of your son. If you succeed, you can go free as air, but if you miss, I will kill you."

While the watching people covered their eyes and trembled with fear, William Tell's son stood straight and still with a big rosy apple on the top of his head. He was afraid, but he trusted his father.

The brave boy did not move, not a muscle, and the arrow sped fast and true. It pierced the apple right through the middle.

Everyone clapped their hands and shouted with joy, except the soldiers and Gessler. The bailiff ground his back teeth and flew into a terrible rage. William Tell had made him look stupid, and he hated him for it.

The soldiers seized William Tell. Gessler said, "I saw you hide another arrow in your shirt. Why did you do that?"

And William Tell answered, "If I had killed my son, that second arrow would have been for you, Gessler."

The bailiff smiled like a tiger. "That was a foolish admission and you will pay for it. I will spare your life but it will bring you no joy. You will be locked up for the rest of your days in the dungeon under my castle."

The soldiers bound William Tell and thrust him into a boat to take him to Gessler's castle on the other side of the lake.

But half way across, the sky darkened and a great wind lashed the lake into a boiling and dangerous ocean.

The soldiers were helpless. Bullies on land, they were timid as mice on the water. They begged Gessler to let them unbind William Tell, who knew how to handle a boat. And, seeing sharp rocks ahead, Gessler screamed out the order.

William Tell stood at the oars.
While the white lightning
split the black sky, and the huge
waves reared up like mountains,
he held the boat steady on course
and rowed hard and strong
through the wild water.

He rowed until he was close to the shore. Then he dropped the oars, grabbed his bow, pushed Gessler aside, and jumped to the bank. He kicked the boat away with his foot and fled from the lake.

The storm was abating. But by the time the soldiers were able to land the boat, they were too late to catch William Tell. He had disappeared, deep in the forest.

William Tell had escaped. But he knew that his friends and his family were now in great danger. Because he had escaped, Gessler would punish them.

There was only one thing to be done. William Tell hid beside the road that led up to the castle. When he saw Gessler, riding proudly on his fine horse, he drew his bow and shot him through the heart. "So perish all tyrants," he cried. "From now on, my land will be free!"

The wicked bailiff was dead.
The joyful news spread from village
to village. It fired the hearts
of the people and stiffened their
courage. For the first time, they
gathered together to attack their
oppressors, and, seeing them so
suddenly fierce and determined,
the Austrian soldiers were
terrified. They ran away in a
panic and the people burned down
their castles.

The people of Schwytz and Uri and Unterwald were grateful to William Tell and his son, who had shown them how to be brave. They all met on the shore of the lake and resolved to be brave themselves in the future. But since each little country alone was too weak to defend itself, they decided to join into one big, new country that would be strong enough to fight for its freedom.

And they called this new country Switzerland.